Dear Parents:

Congratulations! Your child is taking the first steps on an exciting journey. The destination? Independent reading!

STEP INTO READING® will help your child get there. The program offers five steps to reading success. Each step includes fun stories and colorful art or photographs. In addition to original fiction and books with favorite characters, there are Step into Reading Non-Fiction Readers, Phonics Readers and Boxed Sets, Sticker Readers, and Comic Readers—a complete literacy program with something to interest every child.

Learning to Read, Step by Step!

Ready to Read   Preschool–Kindergarten
• big type and easy words • rhyme and rhythm • picture clues
For children who know the alphabet and are eager to begin reading.

Reading with Help   Preschool–Grade 1
• basic vocabulary • short sentences • simple stories
For children who recognize familiar words and sound out new words with help.

Reading on Your Own   Grades 1–3
• engaging characters • easy-to-follow plots • popular topics
For children who are ready to read on their own.

Reading Paragraphs   Grades 2–3
• challenging vocabulary • short paragraphs • exciting stories
For newly independent readers who read simple sentences with confidence.

Ready for Chapters   Grades 2–4
• chapters • longer paragraphs • full-color art
For children who want to take the plunge into chapter books but still like colorful pictures.

STEP INTO READING® is designed to give every child a successful reading experience. The grade levels are only guides; children will progress through the steps at their own speed, developing confidence in their reading. The F&P Text Level on the back cover serves as another tool to help you choose the right book for your child.

Remember, a lifetime love of reading starts with a single step!

For the great-grandchildren
of two wonderful teachers,
Melba and Joseph Membrino
—A.M.

To J.G. for being a star!
—T.B.

Text copyright © 2019 by Anna Membrino
Cover art and interior illustrations copyright © 2019 by Tim Budgen

All rights reserved. Published in the United States by Random House Children's Books,
a division of Penguin Random House LLC, New York.

Step into Reading, Random House, and the Random House colophon are registered trademarks
of Penguin Random House LLC.

Visit us on the Web!
StepIntoReading.com
rhcbooks.com

Educators and librarians, for a variety of teaching tools, visit us at RHTeachersLibrarians.com

Library of Congress Cataloging-in-Publication Data
Names: Membrino, Anna, author. | Budgen, Tim, illustrator.
Title: Big Shark, Little Shark go to school / by Anna Membrino ; illustrated by Tim Budgen.
Description: First edition. | New York : Random House, [2019] | Series: Step into reading. Step 1
Summary: Little Shark is very excited about the first day of school, but Big Shark sleeps late
and they miss the bus.
Identifiers: LCCN 2018052277
ISBN 978-1-9848-9349-9 (trade pbk.) | ISBN 978-1-9848-9350-5 (hardcover library binding) |
ISBN 978-1-9848-9351-2 (ebook)
Subjects: | CYAC: First day of school—Fiction. | Sharks—Fiction.
Classification: LCC PZ7.M5176 Bm 2019 | DDC [E]—dc23

Printed in the United States of America
10 9 8 7 6 5 4 3 2

This book has been officially leveled by using the F&P Text Level Gradient™ Leveling System.

STEP INTO READING®

STEP 1
READY TO READ

Big Shark, Little Shark Go to School

by Anna Membrino

illustrated by Tim Budgen

Random House 🏠 New York

Big shark.

Little shark.

It is morning!

Big Shark is sleepy.

Little Shark is not sleepy.

Little Shark is excited!

It is time
for school!
Little Shark
waits for the bus.

Little Shark

is early.

Little Shark sees the bus!

Where is Big Shark?

13

14

Little Shark swims fast
to Big Shark.

Oh no!

Big Shark is still asleep!

Wake up,
Big Shark!

Little Shark

swims fast.

18

Big Shark

swims fast, too.

Oh no!

The bus is gone!

Little Shark is mad.

Big Shark feels bad.

Wait!

Big Shark

has an idea!

They will ride scooters
to school!

Little Shark

scoots fast.

Big Shark

scoots fast, too.

There is the school!

They even beat the bus!

Now it is time for school!